William Shakespeare, Gabrielle De Nottbeck

Heroines of France

An historic tragedy - in two parts and seven acts

William Shakespeare, Gabrielle De Nottbeck

Heroines of France
An historic tragedy - in two parts and seven acts

ISBN/EAN: 9783337195557

Printed in Europe, USA, Canada, Australia, Japan

Cover: Foto ©Andreas Hilbeck / pixelio.de

More available books at **www.hansebooks.com**

HEROINES OF FRANCE:

AN HISTORIC TRAGEDY,

IN TWO PARTS AND SEVEN ACTS,

BY MISS GABRIELLE DE NOTTBECK.

ARRANGED WITH QUOTED PARTS FROM SHAKESPEARE'S PLAYS,
AND ORIGINAL PARTS BY THE WRITER.

Entered according to Act of Congress, in the year 1877,

By GABRIELLE DE NOTTBECK,

In the office of the Librarian of Congress, at Washington, D. C.

PART I.

PERSONS REPRESENTED.

MARAT,	A French Political Fanatic.
ELISE,	Housekeeper of Marat.
JULIE,	A Servant in Marat's House.
JAQUES,	Valet of Marat.
LENARD,	A Robber.
GRAYMALKIN,	A Witch.
ARMAND CORDAY,	Father of Charlotte.
HENRI CORDAY,	Brother of Charlotte.
ADOLPHE,	Lover of Charlotte.
CHARLOTTE CORDAY,	A Normandy Peasant Girl.

Villagers, Soldiers, Jailors, Priest, Executioner, Etc.

COSTUMES.

The Normandy Peasant Dress.

NOTE.

The play is a true historic tradition, with the exception of a few changes, made to render it a wholesome representation. and is the property of the writer.

HEROINES OF FRANCE.

PART I.

CHARLOTTE CORDAY.

ACT I.

SCENE 1.—*An Open Wood.*

Enter two Villagers.

1st Villager. Look up! Mark yonder dying sun; how like a corpse it looks, whose agony was fierce, whose cries were spent for naught, whose blood like briny waves from a deep sea hath crawled. So sinks it into rest.

2d Villager. Not a fair omen. Yet I trow a bright sun would be mockery; therefore as well to let it frown and speak in honesty, than to set smiles upon the ills to come.—" Men judge by the complexion of the sky, the state and inclination of the day." So, by the frowning of the night, we know what smiles to-morrow he shall wear.

1st Villager. Well, if thou'rt sad, " let's talk of graves, of worms, and epitaphs; make dust our paper, and with rainy eyes, write sorrow on the bosom of the earth."

2d Villager. Nay rather with thy wit turn to a livelier song. But look who comes?

Enter a third Villager.

What! tarrying here? Look there! See how the village burns: lets haste, for in it are our lives. (*Exeunt.*

SCENE II.—*A Village partly burned. Soldiers and Villagers.*

Enter a Villager (rushing among them, who is ADOLPHE.) Our goodly cause fights on our side. "The prayers of holy saints and wrongéd souls, like high-reared bulwarks, stand before our faces." With such array, let's down upon our foes.

The Villagers make a rush toward the Soldiers; they cry, ay! ay! down upon them : down upon them. They fight ; several of the Villagers are slain, HENRI CORDAY *among them ; a few soldiers also slain,* ARMAND CORDAY *is made a prisoner among several other villagers, others escape.)*

(The leader of the band of soldiers repeats an order of MARAT.)

I command, by order of Marat, that all prisoners be now conducted and chained in separate cells, there to await their sentences; advance!

(Soldiers beat drums and the prisoners are led captive. Curtain falls and rises upon the same scene. Villagers come to claim their dead, when the curtain rises they are kneeling and standing by them. CHARLOTTE *is kneeling by the body of her brother, and is the last one to remain.)*

TABLEAU SCENE. *(The first grief of* CHARLOTTE *that leads to her heroic revenge.)*

Charlotte. O noble brow! O head made for a crown! Alas! that none, save one of dust, rests on thee, and yet a crown of dust, fashioned with blood, —with blood that died to save that dust,—is honor's crown, a far more kingly one, of rarer cast than any carvéd one with jewels o'er refinéd gold. *(She suddenly looks up, sees how late it is.)* The dew is falling and the night draws near, and yet not one life with me. Stop! did I say none? Ah! yes, alas! too true; the dead are nothing save in outward view. They, like fine chiselled marble, bear for aye, those black or golden deeds recorded, that can never die! *(She sinks on her brother's form.)* My brother! O my brother!

CURTAIN FALLS.

ACT II.

SCENE I.—*The interior of a cottage.—Charlotte's home.—The body of Henri laid on a bier.—Charlotte weeping by it.*

Adolphe (advancing toward her.) Come, dearest love, weep not; thy tears must cease, or thou, too, Charlotte, shall be made so weak; like a frail lilly by his side thou'lt pine. That well beloved would never have it so. Why vex the dead? Come, dearest, do not weep.

Charlotte (looking up.) Fie! fie for shame! What would'st thou have me do? If thou dost love me save thy land: take up thy sword.

Adolphe. My sword? Where would you send it? It is the tower to guard you, my life : yea, all the manly vigor that I have, are bulwarks—bulwarks, frail ones, to confront such foes ; yet let them dare but look, and these weak arms, like eagles' talons, or like tigers' teeth, shall stick into their marrow and there stay, ere one small finger or a tiny bone relent one atom from its prey.

Charlotte. (*Pointing to her brother's body.*) Then, by the cold, cold damp upon that brow—by those mute lips, no more to utter words—by the high honor that preserves thy steps —by the fond love you bear me—by my love—thou, as a man, go fight them with thy sword ; I, as a woman, shall do all that woman can afford. (*She snatches a dagger from her belt and holds it in the air:* ADOLPHE *makes a rush to seize it from her ; she wrenches away from him.*)

SCENE II. —*A prison cell.*—ARMAND CORDAY *in chains.*

Armand. So in the winter of my ripened age, like a stout icicle that bit the air—like a proud lion of its silver mane, have hunters, vile blood drinkers, chained me here. They fain would smile to see how quick good ice can thaw ; how soon a lion's nature—its bold fire—can die; they fain would mock my homely gown, white hair; so far their mockery have twined their chains. Foul fiends! they knew that honest rags, however worn, can ne'er condemn, but that round coils, though warm from arms of kings, make honor blush, draw tears from strongest men.

Enter a Jailor bearing some food for ARMAND.

Jailor. " O dear discretion, how his words are suited ! The fool hath planted in his mem'ry an army of good words; and I do know a many fools," that stand in worse condition, garnished like him, as steady in their good opinion. (*The jailor puts the bowl on a low bench.*) Come, sip thy broth, t'is good as wine, (*laughs*) Ha ! ha, ha, ha. By Jupiter ! he scorns me for a cook.

Armand. Good man. " For my own part I could be well content." But grief, like a crooked bone, is wedged, it chokes me; therefore, prythee, let me feed on rest.

The Jailor pushes ARMAND *aside.*

Jailor. Away, ungrateful dog, " away you starveling, you elf skin, you dried neat's-tongue," you—(*the jailor goes out, and slams the door of the prison.*)

(ARMAND *stretches himself on a small straw-covered cot near the stand, with bowl.*)

Enter ADOLPHE.

Adolphe. "Why, how now, no greater heart in thee ? Live a little ; comfort a little; cheer thy self a little. Thy conceit is nearer death than thy powers." Thou can'st not live and yet resist from food. " For my sake be comfortable; hold death awhile at the arm's end, I will here be with thee presently; and if I bring thee not something to eat I will give thee leave to die: but, if thou diest before I come, thou art a mocker of my labor. Well said ! thou look'st cheerly: and I'll be with thee quickly and thou shalt not die for lack of a dinner. Cheerly, good father." [*Exeunt.*

9

Enter CHARLOTTE.

Armand. Charlotte, my daughter, wherefore here? My flower—
the flower blooming near my trunk—oh! should she die—should her
sweet beauty spoil by those vile hands—what would her father do?
Why, go stark mad. But wherefore healthy? See I not the truth?
My child, yet not my child. She can but come to me, and that not
oft; I can but see her, cannot keep. Charlotte, no more mine.
Have I no child? My heart stands still, my sight grows dark.
Farewell my child, farewell, farewell, farewell! [*Faints.*

Charlotte. O, father, dear, dear father, do not die; or, if thou
must, wait till I come; wait but one hour—or, if thou can'st, one day.
See what thy child, thy tender girl, can do. (*She bends nearer to him.*)
List, father; thou knowest my friend Elise? (*He revives a little.*) I'll
go to her this night—I'll coax her with a favor very light. Elise, remember what thou said'st. She'll answer, " What, my child?" Thou
promised a wish; that favor when I choose; wilt grant it? She, with
her kindly heart, will say, " Oh, yes." Then I will say, Elise, just let
me go, and in my boldness, so to make a boast, let me go singly, to
thy master's room. I'll only ope' the door, and if he be asleep, creep
in, go round as lightly as a mouse, just make one turn for pride, and
then—(*she hesitates to finish the plan.*)

Armand. (*Without noticing her hesitation, continues.*) Ay, that
sounds cunning, but I see no plan. Well, child, what then?

Charlotte. (*Hesitates, then finally finds courage to reply.*) Before my
shadow shall have crossed that room, by all the saints, by these strong
walls that bind thee, he shall die!

Armand (*surprised.*) My child!—Nay daughter, I'll not have
thee thus imperilled in thy cause. What if another by him?—if within his hand a sword?—What if?—

Charlotte. Nay, father do not fear; all shall go well, and very
well. My plan, spun finer than a spider's web, to be undone, cannot
be without spider's bite. The greatest men and foulest villains shrink
from toads, from serpents, lizards, and all creeping things. I'm
small and shall be one. So good night, father; angels guard thee

till I come. (*They embrace. He, wild in divers thoughts, lets her go. He suddenly comes to and finds her gone—works at the door of cell with all his might to open it.*)

Armand. Charlotte, Charlotte, come back ; my girl, come back ! What have I done—what have I done ? Come back—Come back ! It will not ope'. (*Leaves the door.*) Oh ! had I Samson's strength. These feeble hands can only fold in prayer. (*Kneels.*) Good angels come ; by this hour she is there (*points to heaven.*) Tarry not, but set me loose within yon land so fair. (*Falls dead.*)

Enter ADOLPHE *bringing a small basket of food for* ARMAND.

Adolphe. O, saints ! have mercy ; another gone ! O, poor, poor Charlotte ! 'twill kill her. How can I hide this blast, this cruel cutting grief ? Her dear, dear father ! Now as I think, where has she gone ? O, cruel fate ! wouldst have the blood of all ? Thou dreadful minister, I pray thee, take not all—Oh ! spare my Charlotte !

Enter a JAILOR.

Jailor. 'Tis time I locked thee out ; but for the sake of thy good face, will wait ; so tarry on. (*Sees the body of* ARMAND.) What's this ? Did'st kill him, man ?

Adolphe. Kill him ? Nay, I'd sooner spill each drop of blood that courses in me, than touch him, even with an angry look.

Jailor. Is he thy father ?

Adolphe. All but that. He would have been my father, had not fortune frowned. But where's my Charlotte ?—was she not here ?

Jailor. My service is at later hours. She may have been.

Adolphe. When saw you her the last ?

Jailor. 'Twas yesternight, or, rather ; yesterday just at the setting of the sun.

Adolphe. Did she look calm ?

Jailor hesitates to reply.

Adolphe. Speak, speak, I pray you !

Jailor. Would'st have me tell thee ?

Adolphe. Ay, go on.

Jailor. She looked much as a troubled sea, that rocks long hours before the storm has come. Her breast did heave thus, and her eyes, methinks, if mine are right, were wet.

Adolphe. (*In despair.*) Enough, enough! The storm has come. I hear the thunder, see the flashes fly. O, curses, curses! Where am I—where am I? (*Half wild, he rushes out of the prison.*)

CURTAIN FALLS.

ACT III.

SCENE I.—*An open wood.*

Adolphe. "He jests at scars, that never felt a wound."—But he would weep, who'ld doctor such a sore. (*puts his hand to his heart.*) O, Love, thy darts cut far more deeply in, yea, far more deep, than cruelty can strike. The lover's blindfold eye sees but one scale, and leaves the heavier balance out of sight. And yet a man who never loves at all, is like a pinnacle upon a lonely rock; he hears the music of the lovely waves, but never springs to court them in the caves. For monsters such as he, the whales were raised. By Jupiter! when they do spring, they're gulped and never rise. I need no learnéd doctor medicines or pills. Had I but news of Charlotte, all were well. Who'ed taste of love, must also drink the gall of martyrdom.

Enter LENARD, *a robber, disguised as a peddlar, selling wares.*

Adolphe. Did'st see a pretty maiden on thy way? A girl with flaxen hair and hazel eyes?

Lenard. Ay, she's but a hundred yards behind. (ADOLPHE *runs to find her.*

Enter a VILLAGER.

Lenard. Would'st have a pretty broom to plaster thy good wife with, when it's worn? Or, if thou'rt soft, here's a toy to please thy babe, when graver cares annoy.

Villager. (*laughs*) Ha, ha, ha, ha, old fox, I'll none of them, here's five sous for some snuff.

Lenard. Here, take thy bunch. Blow thy trumpet anywhere save by the bishop's door, he knows me, and if annoyance comes, he'll track me as before.

Villager. I'll pay thee with a cudgel for another warning, be there fifty bishops, or pound thy pasted wares into a hash. Begone thou prowling mongrel of a Jew. (*He pushes* LENARD *forward.* LENARD *turns round upon him.*)

Lenard. Thy first acquaintance with an Israelite, come meet me here at twelve, just on the stroke to night.

Villager. (*he starts thinking it must be the robber* LENARD. *Says aside.*) I wonder if he's Lenard? (*The Villager advances to* LENARD.) I tremble: yet I am no coward—Thou art Lenard.

Lenard. I am.

Villager. May I pass on, or wilt thou hedge my way?

Lenard. (*laughs*) Ha, ha. Thou knowest not Lenard, if thou think'st thou can'st flee. (*he tries to pull a pistol from his belt, the* VILL-AGER *springs upon him and holds him down.*)

Villager. O, I am even with thee, though thou art Lenard. Come I'll be David, thou the Philistine. Thou hast been Philistine for miles around: hast murdered men and women, children, fools in velvets, dames in silks. I now shall be thy slayer, yard for yard. Come, let me bind thee to this oak. (*The* VILLAGER, *with a rope* LENARD *had with his wares, fastens* LENARD *to an oak.* LENARD *struggles to get away from his grasp, but cannot. The* VILLAGER *binds his mouth with a handkerchief.*) Now let me bind the yelling portal of thy throat, so that no trumpet call for thy defense. (*He ties the handkerchief.*) So, so. Now let the vultures pluck thine eyes, the hungry wolves come pay their tribute. (*The* VILLAGER *mocks* LENARD.) How now, Goliath? Would'st have me beg thee leave to pass? Ha, ha, 'tis easy now to cut the shortest road for home. (*Exeunt.*

Enter ADOLPHE *in great distress, not having found* CHARLOTTE.

Adolphe. " I wasted time, and now doth time waste me. For now hath Time made me his numbering clock. My thoughts are minutes, and with sighs. they jar. Their watches on unto mine eyes ; the outward watch, whereto my finger like a dial's point,—is pointing still in cleansing them from tears." (*Turns round, sees* LENARD.) What's this? Lenard, the devil, hanging on a tree? (ADOLPHE *approaches him.*) " On thee, the troubler of the poor world's peace! The worm of conscience still be-gnaw thy soul! No sleep close up that deadly eye of thine, unless it be with some tormenting dream, affrights thee with a hell of ugly devils. Thou elvish-mark'd, abortive, rooting hog! Thou that was sealed in thy nativity, the slave of nature and the son of hell! Thou slander of thy heavy mother's womb! Thou loathed issue of thy father's loins! Thou rag of honour! Thou detested." (ADOLPHE *sees some one passing down a road, turns first, and stabs* LENARD, *then goes to on his way.*)

Adolphe. Here take this rough farewell before 1 go. (ADOLPHE *stabs* LENARD. *goes on his way.*

ACT IV.

SCENE 1.—*House of* MARAT *in Paris,* ELISE *sitting sewing in the court yard.*—CHARLOTTE, *coming from a distance advances to her.*

Charlotte. When bees are busy they are always kind. "How doth the busy bee each shining hour, improves it at the utmost of its power." So working bees of course are good, because to work it is a virtue. So my Elise is, as she always was, good. (*Stoops and kisses her.*) Are you going to sit here long Elise ?

Elise. Awhile; come sit by me; thy face looks warm—the breeze will cool thee.

Charlotte. Gladly so, 'twill suit my purpose. But, dear Elise, (*she draws her work as if to take it from her*—ELISE *gently resists her*) stop old wive's work; I'd chat with thee.

Elise. Speak on my child.

Charlotte. Art angry Elise ?

Elise. (*Bends toward* CHARLOTTE, *kisses her.*) Nay, now, thou'rt in a fooling mood. Why child, I never loved thee better.

Charlotte. Then wilt thou grant a favor ?

Elise. Should it not weigh beyond my power, most gladly.

Charlotte. May I go to the Blue-room—just look in ? I never saw it, save with thee one day I spied it through the key-hole.

Elise. My master's ill. I dare not let thee near at such a time.

Charlotte. Oh ! I'll go lightly as a bird, and if he be asleep 'twould surely do no harm just to creep in, and hurry out. Thou knowest, when thou sickened at my home, how I did pass thee when asleep and never woke thee.

Elise. Well I may grant, since good should be rewarded, thou shalt be, for now I mind me what thou did'st for me. Go child, if that can please thee.

Charlotte. Oh ! thanks, thanks, my true, my loving Elise. Tarry till I come, for I would fain be near thee when I've done. (*Exeunt*

Enter JULIE, *a servant, coming from a basement, carrying a bowl with partly peeled carrots.*

Julie. (*she calls.*) Elise, Elise.

Elise. What is it, Julie?

Julie. I've stolen from my work a bit, to come and tell thee of a dream, a dreadful dream, mixed with a nightmare, that I had last night.

Elise. Well, come, let's hear it. (JULIE *comes and sits by* ELISE. *peels her carrots, and tells the dream.*)

Julie. I dreamt I saw a field with scorpions, aligators, toads ; all sorts of vermin, rats, and bats, and mice. And as I nearer went. I saw thy friend, thy tender Charlotte, battling with a snake. The snake, it hissed and curled, but the brave girl with her soft hands, did clasp its neck. It writhed, and tried to sting, but still she held, Then faint for want of air, it gasped and gasped, till with one leap, it broke from her, and breathed its last.

Elise. No ill will come. 'Twas only the ravings of thy heated mind. Thou knowest Julie, how too big a drop of Hock can hurt thee.

Julie. Nay, 'twas no Hock, Moselle or other wine; I've steadily drunk ale since Michaelmas.

Elise. Oh Julie, Julie.

Julie. Ask Father Claire, I tell him my confessions.

Elise. Well I believe thee, take my hand for it. (*They shake hands.*

Julie. Well met, well met. Dissevered friendship never can be healed, or if it is, 'tis like a mended pot. Never all smooth, all blended as of yore, but with an ugly seam that never was before. (ELISE *turns round, sees behind her a fiddler and a man with a trained bear. The bear can be a man dressed up in furs to look like that animal, having a bear's head mask, with a strap muzzle.* ELISE *shrieks.*)

The man with bear. Don't be afraid Madame, the bear's as gentle as a lamb. Come Bruno be a gentleman, show what a pretty bow thou can'st salute with. (*The bear bows.*) Now let us have a waltz. Come Bruno, come. (*They waltz, the fiddle strikes up a tune.*) Now run get thee a partner for a minuet, while'st I go muster others for the dance. (*The bear runs toward* JULIE, JULIE *and* ELISE *terrified, run skrieking toward the house, and make good their escape. The fiddler and the man with bear in fits of laughter. The men call Bruno and leave.*

Enter ELISE, *she comes back to get her work, then goes to the porch, looks through the bars of the gate, down the street.*

Elise. " That way the noise is.—Tyrant show thy face :" I ween 'tis not with all thou'd play such games. I would that thou wert slain, thou and thy bear, that babes and timid women might have peace. (ELISE *stands looking down the street. A French Peasant woman comes up to her and says, through the gate :*

Peasant woman. Elise, "tu as esté en Angleterre, et tu parles bien le language."

Elise. " Un peu, Madame."

Peasant woman. " Je te prie m'enseignez ; il faut que j ápprenne á parler. Comment appelez vous la main en Anglois ? "

Elise. " La main ? elle est appeleé de hand."

Peasant woman. " De hand. Et les doigts ?

Elise. " Les doigts ? ma foy, je oublie les doigts; mais je me souviendray. Les doigts, je pense qui ils sont appelés de fingres ouy de fingres."

Peasant woman. " La main, de hand; les doigts, de fingres. Je pense que je suis bon escolier. J'ay gagné deux mots d'Anglois vistement comment appelez vous les ongles ? "

Elise. " Les ongles? les appelons de nails."

Peasant woman. " De nails. Escoutez, dites moy si je parle bien ; de hand, de fingres, de nails."

Elise. " C'est bien dit, madame; il est fort bon Anglois."

Peasant woman. " Dites moi l'Anglois pour le bras."

Elise. " De arm, madame."

Peasant woman. " Et le coude ? "

Elise. " De elbow."

Peasant woman. " Escoutez moy Elise, escoutez. De hand, de fingre, de nails, de arm, de bilbow."

Elise. " De elbow, madame."

Peasant woman. " Oh je m'en oublie; die elbow. Comment appelez vous le col ?"

Elise. " De neck, madame."

Peasant woman. " De nick: Et le menton ?"

Elise. " De chin."

Peasant woman. " De sin. Le col, de nick, le menton, de sin."

Elise. " Ouy Sauf votre honneur en vérité vous ' parlez ' aussi droict que les natifs d'Angleterre."

Peasant woman. " Je ne doute point d'apprendre en peu de temps."

Elise. " N'avez vous pas déjà oublié ce que je vous ay enseignée?''

Peasant woman. " Non. De hand, de fingre, de mails."

Elise. " De nails, madame."

Peasant woman. " De nails, de arme, de illbow."

Elise. " Sauf votre honneur, de elbow."

Peasant woman. " Ainsi dis je. De elbow, de nick, et de sin."

Elise. " Excellent, madame."

Peasant woman. " De hand, de fingre, de nails, de arm, de elbow, de nick, de sin. C'est assey pour une fois " merci, madame, merci. Je me sauve pour disner. Au révoir.

Elise. Au révoir, madame.

The Peasant woman goes on her way. ELISE stands looking down the street.

CURTAIN FALLS.

ACT V.

SCENE I. —*Charlotte in a passage-way leading to* MARAT'S *room.*

Charlotte. " It will have blood; they say, blood will have blood; stones have been known to move, and trees to speak: Augurs, and understood relations, have by magot-pies, and choughs, and rooks, brought forth the secret'st man of blood."—O! Many an old man's sigh, and many a widow's, and many an orphan's water standing eye.—Men for their sons', wives for their husbands', and orphans for their parents' timeless death, " Have" rued the hour ever thou wast born--The owl shrieked at thy birth, an evil sign; the night-crow cried aboding luckless time; dogs howled, and hideous tempests shook the trees. The raven rock'd her on the chimney's top and chattering pies in dismal discord sung.—Teeth had'st thou in thy head when thou wast born, to signify thou cam'st to bite the world! (*She rushes forward a few steps as if* MARAT *were under her and she stabbing him.*) Down, down to hell; and say I sent thee thither.—See how my sword weeps "for revenge!" " O, may such purple tears be always shed," flow down until revenge is bought! (*She advances till she comes to* MARAT'S *door, looks round to see if anyone is near. Listens at his door.*) How still—all dead—in silence—save myself; but oh! my heart it leaps, leaps as though struggling to desert me. Yet the heart is truer to one's self than aught. Than aught, e'en though a monster, a warrior 'gainst all other hearts it prove. Heart to heart is not all mixed with love, such close communion dives as deep in hate as ever in the fields where tender passion dreams. Now for the hour! Mount up, my soul, mount up! Thy courage dare not slack. Mount up my fury! Need 1 whip it up? Hate boils itself, nor needs one coal to feed it!

SCENE II.—*The Blue room.* MARAT *wrapped with a robe, on a couch.* —*A very dim light burning.*

Enter CHARLOTTE.

Charlotte. He sleeps: 'tis well. First let the tiger lick its jaw, and choose what side 'twill turn upon its prey: then with a leap, spring on it: and the work is o'er! 'Tis a foul victim for a goodly meal. A sickly prey dies quick ; 'tis better so. My prize is only in thy death. not in thy carcase save to spit on it. (*She advances, lays the dagger against his cheek; he turns, disturbed in sleep, and says, as if in a dream :*)

Marat. What cold was that that chilled me ? I am wrapped. Death never comes so near, then passes on. Sure, if it was death's hand, it only stroked ; that is a gentle way, then why not sleep ? Why should I not sleep as before ? Enough of trouble when it bustles at the door. (*He begins to sleep,* CHARLOTTE *rouses him.*)

Charlotte. 'Tis come foul villain. Think you mercy will be kind ? Where is the mercy thou did'st show to man ?

Marat. (*Starts up.*) What's this ? 'Tis not a dream. My senses sleep not. I am full awake. (*He tries to find out what disturbed him; he sees* CHARLOTTE.) Who art thou ? Angel, devil, or tormenting ghost ?

Charlotte. I'm none, yet live for all. I live to work out vengeance for dead men ; I live to kill a devil in his prime ; I live my work to crown when done—ay, e'en the angels shall look down and smile.

Marat. Come, can a woman ever raise a hand 'gainst man ?

Charlotte. Ay, so think men till virtue proves she can.

Marat. Where is thy gentle heart ? The tender heart of woman, thou can'st show no pity ?

Charlotte. Pity ! Monster, how cam'st thou by that word ? Beelzebub it was who taught thee. Show me his dictionary. Pity is not there. Pity ? Look in my eye. wretch, read it there. Look in : behold the father and the brother of this germ. They cried to thee for pity; thou had'st none. Know then that pity, ay pity no longer shall implore. Justice is waiting till death hath open for thee hell's dark door. (MARAT *shrieks for help; tries to pull the bell cord.* CHARLOTTE *springs upon him, and with a dagger stabs* MARAT.)

Charlotte. Too late! too late! Die, villain, die!   (*Exeunt.*)

Enter JAQUES, *valet of* MARAT.

Jaques. Murdered! Nay, he hath killed himself. His sufferings, I ween, were too intense. So let him lie. (*Spreads the robe neatly over the body.*) I'll search this matter, though it cost my running legs till Doomsday.

Enter ELISE.

Elise. (*Shrinking back at the sight of the corpse.*) Dead! dead! Can he be dead?

Jaques. Ay, even so. Now, by the saints, I mind me of a girl, a stranger. What did she with you? (*The truth flashes on* ELISE, *but to save herself and* CHARLOTTE *she hides her emotion under a pretended fear of* JAQUES.)

Elise. (*Terrified by* JAQUES.) Why, Jaques you frighten me. Have you gone mad? A friend may see a friend, that's naught amiss. You saw the girl; she came to while an idle hour here.

Jaques. Nay, she did while no hour with thee, for I myself did let her in. Then, won by her sweet face, I, for excuse, did sit by thee ten minutes after she had come. Then hastily back to my work returned. What was it? A whistle, a knock, did call me? At that time she had gone.

Elise. Well, what of that? A bird may light and wish to linger on a bough; something may come affright. divert it sooner from its place. E'en so might she have for a reason left.

Jaques. Did'st know her reason?

Elise. Nay.

Jaques. Dost swear thy nay ?

Elise. I do.

Jaques. Then I'll not tarry ; too long have I delayed ; the foe has fled. Saints, send me in you aid. (*Exeunt.*

SCENE III.—*A street in Paris.* CHARLOTTE *led down the street by two officers.* ADOLPHE *from a side street rushes to her.*

Adolphe. Good saints what do I see ? Charlotte ! Charlotte ! Can it be Charlotte ? (CHARLOTTE, *at the sound of his voice, faints, he runs and stabs one of the officers in the back, the officer falls dead. He then fights with the other officer and finally kills him also.* CHARLOTTE *revives and calls for help.*

Charlotte. Help ! Help ! good citizens. Help ! Help ! (*A crowd gather round them, but are afraid to interfere.* ADOLPHE *stabs the officer and makes his escape with* CHARLOTTE.) (*Exeunt.*) (*The crowd stand looking at the body of the officer. An officer comes to see what is the cause of the crowd, from his post in a further part of the city.*

Officer. What's this ? Come wag your tongues ! Are ye such cowards that ye dar'nt speak ? (*A clownish boy in the crowd screams.*)

Boy. Hold peace in gratefulness, your liver's saved. (*The officer in a rage tries to break through the crowd to get at him, the crowd prevent the officer.*)

Officer. Here you sleek puppy, let me cut your tongue. (*The officer then turns to the crowd and says :*) Is this the defense to give the Capitol when matters stir up wrong ? Fie ! fie ! ye mongrels, ye cross bred curs of France. Have devils tied you dumb? (*The crowd rush upon him and push toward a side street.*)

Crowd. Enough ! Enough ! Let's collar him ! Let's collar him. (*Exeunt.*

(*Men, women and children are seen in the streets. Several women carrying baskets with vegetables or fruit. Children playing.*)

(Enter a man with a bill, sticks it to a post. The bill reads thus :
500 francs reward.—For the arrest of CHARLOTTE CORDAY, *murderess*
of MARAT. *Signed by order of the Police; Headquarters, Rue St. An-*
toine, Paris. August.) ˝˝ .

(A man passing along the street goes up to the sign, reads it.)

Man. O! horrid picture of a death to come.   And yet " I thank
thee who hast taught my frail mortality to know itself; and by those
fearful objects to prepare this body like to them, to what I must.
For death rememberéd should be like a mirror, who tells us life's but
breath, to trust it, error."   I trust my death will never come by such
a road.   *(He shivers at the thought, and goes on his way : he looks so*
miserable a good hearted fisherman has pity on him.)

Fisherman.   How now, how now, is it "Black Monday" with thee?
Man.   No, blacker than all days, I never saw a gold day yet.
Fisherman.   Hast ever been at sea?
Man.   When a boy, methinks I once was there.
Fisherman   " Can'st thou catch any fishes then ? "
Man.   " I never practised it."
Fisherman.   " Nay, then thou wilt starve sure ; for here's nothing
to be got now a days, unless thou fish for't."
Man.   " What I have been, I have forgot to know ; but what I
am, want teaches me to think on.   A man throng'd up with cold :
my veins are chill, and have no more of life than may suffice to give
my tongue the heat to ask your help, which if you shall refuse, when
I am dead, for what I am a man, pray see me buried."
Fisherman.   " Die, quoth-a?   Now gods forbid!   I have a gown
here : come, put it on, keep thee warm.   Now, afore me a handsome
fellow!   Come. thou shalt go home. and we'll have flesh for holidays.
fish for fasting days, and moreo'er, puddings and flap-jacks; and thou
shalt be welcome."
Man.   I thank you sir.   " Thanks. Fortune, yet after all my crosses.
thou givest me somewhat to repair myself.   Where with it, I may

appear a gentleman." I'll go find a trade. "And if that my low fortune's better, I'll pay your bounties; till then rest your debtor." (*They shake hands. Exeunt.*)

(*Enter a man in the street, he finds a small bundle which is a crushed letter.*)

Man. Ho, ho! What's this treasure floating in the dust? No diamonds, pearls or rubies. (*Laughs.*) Ha, ha, ha, ha, I'll warrant 'tis some lover's jewel though. A bit of poetry. Tut. tut. Senti mentality. Ha, ha, ha, ha, of course. A piece about the heart. Ha, ha, ha, ha. What could dig closer to the heart? (*He reads the verses.*)

THE HEART.

How oft it flutters like a bird,
All trembling with delight;
How oft the drops from galling tears
Have left a bow at night;—
A bow, whose red, whose blue, whose green,
Too hidden were, though, to be seen.

O, could each draw the misty veil
That wraps another's heart,
How much of joy, how much of pain
Would linger or depart.

How much of love we thought was ours
We'd find a treasure flown:
Then tears and sighs no more need ask
Why turned that heart to stone.

'Tis some Ophelia wrote this for her Hamlet. I'll be pale Hamlet, till Hamlet comes for it. (*A band of soldiers pass down a street, he runs with the crowd after it.*)

SCENE IV.—CHARLOTTE *in a wood by a cave, an old witch beside her.*

Charlotte. " O, where is" Adolphe, "saw you him to-day ? "

Witch. " Madame, an hour before the worshipp'd sun peeréd forth the golden window of the east, a troubled mind drave me to walk abroad. Where, underneath the grove of sycamore, that westward rooteth from the city's side—so early walking—did I see your "love." Towards him I made; but he was 'ware of me, "although he knew. me not." And stole into the covert of the wood. I measuring his "feelings" by my own,—that most are busied when they are most alone, —pursued my humor, not pursuing his, and gladly shunnéd who gladly fled from me."

Charlotte. (*Sighs.*) " Ah, me, sad hours seem long." O, would I had sent word by thee.

Witch. " Hie to your" cave, " I'll find" Adolphe "to comfort you."

Charlotte. O, bid him come, yet grieve him not with how I pined for him. Go, good witch, go.

Witch. Ay, ay, I'll go, if he be in the wood, I'm sure to find him ; so farewell lady, till I fetch thy Love.

Charlotte. Farewell, farewell, until thou bring him here. " Is there no pity sitting in the clouds, that sees into the bottom of my grief.' O, fortune, fortune! all men call thee fickle, what dost thou with him that is renowned for faith ? Be fickle, fortune; for then, I hope thou wilt not keep him long, but send him." (*She goes in the cave.*)

Enter ADOLPHE, *with a gun, wearing a game-bag at his side, filled with birds.*

Adolphe. Her spies, like thirsty blood-hounds, track the ground. Their " murderous shaft that's shot, hath not yet lighted. (*He looks toward the cave where* CHARLOTTE *is secreted.*) And now our safest way is to avoid the aim." O, curse them. " A plague upon them !

Wherefore should I curse? Would curses kill, as doth the mandrake's groan, I would invent as bitter searching terms, as curst, as harsh, and horrible to hear, delivéred strongly through my fixéd teeth, with full as many signs of deadly hate, as leanéd-faced Envy in her loathsome pit." "My tongue should stumble in her earnest words; mine eyes should sparkle, like the beaten flint; my hair be fixed on end, as one distract; ay, every joint should seem to curse and ban; and, even now, my burdened heart would break, should I not curse them. Poison be their drink! Gall, worse than gall, the daintiest that they taste! Their sweetest shade a grove of cypress trees! Their chiefest prospect, murdering basilisks! Their softest touch, as smart as lizard stings! Their music frightful as the serpent's hiss; and boding owls make the concert full! All the foul terrors in dark seated hell "—

(CHARLOTTE *comes from the cave, rushes out when she sees* ADOLPHE, ADOLPHE *rushes to her.*)

Charlotte. Adolphe! Adolphe! (*They embrace.*)

Adolphe. "Foul whisperings are abroad; but let's be bold and resolute:—laugh to scorn. Be lion-mettled, proud; and take no care. Who chafes and frets" is ever first to fall. Let's hie us, with best courage, from this place. Like birds who leave their nest, desert this cave; and let who will come in and take his rest. (*They make a move to depart; the witch, coming from the cave, calls.*)

Witch. Stay, children, stay. Come, Adolphe, lend an ear to me. (*She leads* ADOLPHE. CHARLOTTE *goes back in the cave. The* WITCH *leads* ADOLPHE *to another old hag, Mother* "GRAYMALKIN," *who is stirring a mess in a cauldron. The first witch departs.* "GRAYMALKIN" *sings over the cauldron.*)

> " Round about the cauldron go;
> In the poisoned entrails throw.
> Toad, that under cold stone,
> Days and nights hast thirty-one.
> Boil thou first i' the charméd pot;
> Sweltered venom sleeping got,
> Double, double toil and trouble,
> Fire, burn : and cauldron bubb'e."

26

(*The hag sees* ADOLPHE. ADOLPHE *shrinks in horror from her.*)

"*Graymalkin.*" "Good sir, why do you start: and seem to fear ?"

Adolphe. (*aside.*) "This supernatural soliciting" can bring no good.
If ill, why should I stay ? It may buy curses; then, why not away ?
I'll 'bide no longer. Good-day, good witch, good-day. (*He turns
to leave.*)

"*Graymalkin.*" Nay stay ; I prithee stay.

Adolphe. Hast thou a prophecy ?

"*Graymalkin.*" Ay. A grave and timely warning for thee.

Adolphe. Speak on I pray.

"*Graymalkin.*" (*She draws a chart oracle from under a stone.*) Draw
near, look on. Mark how the needle points. There lies the road
that thou did'st meditate to fly with Charlotte. (ADOLPHE *starts.*)
See there the beards, the staves, and hungry knives. (ADOLPHE
shudders, the witch pats ADOLPHE *on the shoulder, he kneeling beside
her.*) Come boy, list to my riper wisdom. (*She draws from her
pocket a long white veil.*) Here, take this to thy Charlotte ; forbid
her more to wander from the cave, save when the white moon pales
just on the stroke of twelve. Her spies will think she is a ghost, and
for their lives will turn and take to heels. (ADOLPHE *laughs.*)

Adolphe. Ha ha, Ha ha. How fine, like gold hid in a buried
mine has been thy wit ! 'Twould take three-headed foxes to un-
earth thy plan.

"*Graymalkin.*" Ay, trust me; that it would.

Adolphe. There take this coin for thy trouble, and here (*he draws
a bird from his game bag*) this fatted bird to feed thy liver.

"*Graymalkin.*" I thank you sir. If trouble comes again, remember
Graymalkin.

Adolphe. Ay, that I will. I now must hie me to my Charlotte.
Good-day, Dame " Graymalkin."

"Graymalkin." Good-day, kind sir, good-day. (ADOLPHE *goes on his way, the witch goes back to her cauldron, and continues her song.*

> " Fillet of a fenny snake
> In the cauldron boil and bake:
> Eye of newt, and toe of frog,
> Wool of bat, and tongue of dog,
> Adder's fork, and blind-worm's sting.
> Lizard's leg, and owlet's wing,
> For a charm to soothe all trouble,
> Bubble, bubble, boil and bubble,
> " Double, double toil and trouble.
> Fire burn, and Cauldron" hiss.

SCENE V.—*An open wood. Midnight.* CHARLOTTE, *like a Ghost, with the veil entirely covering her, wanders round the wood. A thunder storm comes, the rain wets the veil; the charm is broken; her foes recognize her features and detect her scheme. They arrest her. In order to give the effect desired of the veil wet, the veil that hung loose before should be drawn tightly down over the face when the storm begins.*

Enter a Robber.

Robber. (*Calls.*) " What ho! What ho! What ho!" (*He takes out a whistle, and whistles for a signal.*

Enter two Robbers.

1*st Robber.* Come, lets' go search our gold; come, come; 'twas 'neath yon rock I buried it. (*The Robbers go toward the rock; when they come there,* CHARLOTTE *is standing on it.*) " Peace; break thee off." Look, ~~look~~,—look on,—look there.

2*d Robber.* (*Starts.*) " It harrows me with fear;" methinks it is a ghost.

3d Robber. " See, it stalks away." (CHARLOTTE *leaves the rock ; comes back to it just as the men are about to roll it away to find their gold.*)

1st Robber. (*Looks up, sees* CHARLOTTE.) By Jupiter, look up ; why here it comes again. (CHARLOTTE *comes nearer. Two of the Robbers tremble and run off; the first Robber slowly retreats from the place, and stands looking at her.*) Methinks it is a miser spirit, would bar us from our goods. What ever 'tis " truly I do fear it ! Yet," "what man dare, I dare ! Approach thou, like the rugged Russian bear, the armed rhinoceros, or the *Hyrcan* tiger. Take any shape but that, and my firm nerves shall never tremble : or be alive again." " Hence, horrible shadow !" (CHARLOTTE *disappears.*) " Unreal mockery, hence !—Why, so !—being gone, I am a man again." (*He rolls back the rock and takes out the bag of gold.*) Ha ! Ha ! my pretty coins ! I'd wade again another frightful sea before I'd lose your golden faces. (*He takes the bag of gold, goes on his way.*) Now, back I'll go and join my chicken-livered hounds. (*Sings.*)

> O, tell me what is like to wealth,
> Like to wealth, like to wealth ;
> O, tell me what is like to wealth,
> And a —

(*He starts,* CHARLOTTE *appears again, face to face with him ; he trembles, drops the bag, and runs off. Thunder is heard—a heavy thunder storm breaks upon the scene.*)

Charlotte. Alas ! alas ! What shall I do ? Where can I go ? What shall I do ? The very heavens war against me. " Are there no stones in heaven, but what serve " for plunder ? " O, insupportable. O heavy hour ! Methinks it should be now a huge eclipse of sun and moon, and that the affrighted globe did yawn at alteration." —What noise is this ? " The noise was high." Hark ! Hark ! (*Men break through the wood, who are spies on* CHARLOTTE. CHAR-

LOTTE *sees the men, she shrieks.*) What shall I do? What shall I do? I am unarmed, defenceless; my veil no longer can protect. The cruel, heavy rain hath crushed my shield. Once more I'm in my natural helpless state, a bleeding deer, that's hunted by the foe. (*She runs wildly, shrieking. the men running upon her tracks; they lead her off, captive.*

Enter ADOLPHE, *he sees* CHARLOTTE'S *veil on the ground; picks it up.*

Adolphe. Black ministers of night, what do I see! Her veil? Wheres. Charlotte? Had she life, she'd wear it. Have wolves devoured? Nay, 'tis August. No wolves devour in summer time. (*He sees the bag of gold on the ground.*) Alack, alack, it is some other wolves; see there the bulbous remnant of their tracks. O Charlotte! Charlotte! Perhaps this hideous bundle will betray, (*he picks up the bag*) will give some scent to lead me on their way. (*He opens it.*) Gold, yellow gold. How came they to have held with such a girlish grasp? How dear had gold been once to me and mine. Did ever man breathe yet, who smiled not at its hue? Yet, bright and precious as sweet gold it is, I'd rather cut my soul from out its seat, than touch one coin from such guilty hands. (*He throws down the bag.*) Away, away! Like as the ocean vomits up its pearls, so to the earth I fling their cursed ore!

SCENE VI.—CHARLOTTE *in prison, sitting on a low stool, wiping her tears.*

Charlotte. They say that trials sanctify the mind; or else so sour it it turns to wrong. The tender deer that loves to lick the hand, may on the morrow face the hand and butt. Ay, that is bitter; but not worst of all. 'Tis not the ghostly fire of despair. (*As she raises her hand to her brow, a stray lock goes with it. She sees her hair has turned white; she shrieks.*) My hair white! turned in a night!

Enter ADOLPHE *rushing to her.*

Adolphe. My Charlotte! (*Blank with wonder, he holds her before him.*)

Charlotte. Do you not know me? (ADOLPHE *bows his head, and weeps.*)

Charlotte. Nay, do not grieve. Oh! far, far better to be born, born cursed now; now wear the crown; now drag the heavy cross; now be cut up; now stoned; than to be nursed on fatted meats, drink wines, die on a rosy bed; then wake like baited worms to writhe for aye.

Adolphe. "O woe! O woeful, woeful day! Most lamentable day, most woeful day. That ever, ever, I did yet behold! O day! O day! O day! O hateful day! Never was seen so black a day as this; O woeful, woeful day!"

Charlotte. (*She turns to him; they embrace.*) Adolphe! Adolphe! (*He rushes from her, and runs to a corner where he sees a bottle. The bottle contains a deadly mixture; he goes back to her; he tries to open the bottle.*)

Adolphe. See, Charlotte, see. Without despair, I never had contrived; 'tis only saints and fools when barriers intervene, submissively will yield, put on the yoke, then hive. (*He embraces* CHARLOTTE.) Dear, dear Charlotte, thy death I cannot stay, but can be chooser of the instrument.

Charlotte. O Adolphe! Adolphe! (ADOLPHE *suddenly starts and runs to the window.*)

Adolphe. What's the hour? 'Tis five; the gates of Day just creaking 'ere they spring. Oh! would I had the strength to roll back time, or mighty finger to hold still this hour.—This bitter, bitter hour, yet honied golden one beside to come. (*Goes back toward* CHAR-LOTTE, *finds her sitting, weeping. He has in his hand a handkerchief, with some of the deadly mixture from the bottle he found poured upon it. Pours more on it as he advances. He intends to let* CHARLOTTE *have*

*an easy death and escape the block. He makes several efforts to kill
her, finally holds it to her till she falls.*)

Adolphe. (*He goes toward* CHARLOTTE *with the handkerchief in his
hand. She does not see him as her face is buried in her hands while
she is weeping.*) O, not all the curling, biting flames of hell; the long
eternity without an end; Unscabbered swords, or fearful, horrid
sights;—could buy such torture as to take her life. O, how my
strength grows weak, my senses numb. Before I blow that light,
this spirit shall have flown. Are there no angels, or vile spirits of the
air, in mercy, for one moment, can look down? Look down, just
spare one inch of passing Time, to let a sword or mighty cutlass fall
to seal our deaths, end let Death crown it all? But time doth fly,
and words cry out in vain. So then, yes then, so let her death come
quick; ay, quick before she rise. 'Tis merciful, oh, most merciful as
so! No minutes now. Come hands and do your work. In killing,
ye but prove unfathomable love. (*He rushes to* CHARLOTTE, *holds
the handkerchief firmly to her face. She sinks back apparently lifeless
in his arms. He lays her gently on the floor. He looks at her.*) "Alack
the day; she's dead, she's dead. Ha! let me see her. (*He feels her
hands.*) Out alas! she's cold; her blood is settled, and her joints are
stiff. Life and these lips" are " separated." Death lies on her, like
an untimely frost upon the sweetest flower of the field. O lamentable day! O woeful time! O me, O me!—"My love, my only life,
revive, look up, or I will die with thee." 'Tis done! 'tis done! No
more to be undone. O, Charlotte, Charlotte, Charlotte. (*He sinks
weeping beside her.*)

CURTAIN FALLS.

ACT VI.

The curtain rises upon the same scene. ADOLPHE *does not appear; he is so heart broken, he cannot come among the villagers who appear on the scene to mourn over* CHARLOTTE, *whom they think dead. Several maidens, with flowers, come. One of the villagers takes up the body of* CHARLOTTE *from the floor and lays it on a cot in the prison; the maidens strew the flowers over her, while the villagers, with instruments, play a low requiem. One of the maidens sings a dirge.*

DIRGE.

" Fear no more the heat of the sun,
        Nor the winter's rages ;
Thou thy worldly task hast done.
        Home art gone, and ta'en thy wages:

CHORUS.—Golden lads and girls all must,
        As chimney- sweepers, come to dust.
" Fear no more the frown o' the great,
        Thou are past the tyrant's stroke;
Care no more to clothe and eat ;
        To thee the reed is as the oak.

CHORUS.—The sceptre, learning physic must
        All follow this, and come to dust."
" Fear no more the lightning flash ;
        Nor the all dreaded thunder tone ;
Fear not slander, censure rash :
        Thou hast finished joy and moan ;

CHORUS.—All lovers young, all lovers must,
                Consign to thee and come to dust."

SCENE II. (CHARLOTTE, *between the first and second scene, has revived, the poison not having killed her, but merely having put her in an insensible state. CHARLOTTE appears, dressed in white, led by* ADOLPHE. *The priest in front of them, villagers and a crowd following behind. They march to the block, which is on an open square, where the Executioner is waiting. A few Soldiers are stationed to prevent a riot.*

ADOLPHE. (*Embraces* CHARLOTTE, *leads her towards the block, pauses, and says*) To pay the penalty for right can bring no pain [*the crowd cheer him, a soldier points a rifle at him; the leader of the soldiers prevents him from firing.*] Shine out, fair sun! Where are your smiles? Charlotte goes but to sleep: among first wakers to awake again! (*He embraces* CHARLOTTE, *afterwhich she waves a farewell to the Villagers.* ADOLPHE *falls fainting.*]

CURTAIN FALLS.

JOAN OF ARC.

PERSONS REPRESENTED.

French Side.

CHARLES, DAUPHIN, KING OF FRANCE.

REIGNIER, DUKE OF ANJOU.

THE DUKE OF ALENCON.

THE BASTARD OF ORLEANS.

THE GHOST OF JOAN OF ARC'S MOTHER.

JOAN OF ARC, a Shepardess of the Village of Domremi, on the border of the Meuse.

English Side.

THE DUKE OF BEDFORD.

EARL TALBOT.

THE DUKE OF BURGUNDY.

THE DUKE OF YORK.

French Soldiers, English Soldiers, etc.

NOTE.

At the time of these battles, Henry the Sixth is on the throne of England.

HEROINES OF FRANCE:

PART II.

JOAN OF ARC.

ACT VII.

SCENE I. – *An open wood, a small chapel in it.* JOAN OF ARC *asleep under a tree opposite the chapel. The ghost of* JOAN'S *mother appears in the chapel.* JOAN, *waking up, sees it.*

Joan. (*Waking up, looks toward the chapel, and advances toward it.*) What's that? What's that? Some wretched spirit broken from its grave. See how it beckons. I've done harm to none, why should it call? (*She goes nearer, shrieks.*) My Mother! 'Tis my mother! (*She grows calmer, and looks at her.*)

The Ghost of Joan's Mother. Joan! My daughter!

Joan. O gracious mother, thou knowest how I love thee. Spare me, mother, and leave me yet my life. I love the world; I love my life; though I have mourned for thee, my raining tears have laved me mornings, nights, for weeks, for months in sorrow, for thee: but, oh! I cannot come. Mother, O spare me yet; my gentle mother come not as the fearful herald of my death. (*She shrieks.*) I cannot die! I will not, will not die!

The Ghost of Joan's Mother.) Fear not, Joan, 'tis thy life I bring. Thou art a virgin that was formed by heaven, to be a woman captain —a leader among men. France dies without thee. So buckle on an armor, take a sword; bid Domremi farewell; hie to the king, tell him what thou hast seen, and trust me Joan he shall let thee go.

Joan. Ay, ghostly mother, I shall go. France, bleeding France, is calling; I'll away; nor shall this small arm rest till it hath felled each foe! (*The Ghost of* JOAN's *Mother vanishes.* JOAN *hies to the king.*)

SCENE II.—*The Village of Domremi. When the curtain rises, a troop of soldiers in a file on each side of the stage, are playing the " Marsellaise."* JOAN *enters, dressed in a steel armor, like a man, with a short white tunic, with a blue sash belt: she is mounted on a steed, richly harnessed.*

Enter the Bastard of "Orleans."

Bastard of Orleans. "Where's the Prince Dauphin, I have news for him."

King Charles. "Bastard of Orleans, thrice welcome to us."

Bast. "Methinks your looks are sad; your cheer appalled. Hath the late overthrow wrought this offence? Be not dismayed, for succour is at hand: A holy maid hither with me I bring. Which, by a vision sent to her from heaven, ordained is to raise this tedious siege, and drive the English forth the bounds of France. The spirit of deep prophecy she hath. Exceeding the nine sibyls of old Rome; what's past, and is to come, she can descry. Speak, shall I 'bring' her in? Believe my words, for they are certain and infallible."

King Charles. "Go call her in. (*Exit Bastard.*) But first to try her skill. REIGNIER stand thou as Dauphin in my place. Question her proudly; let thy looks be stern:—By this means we shall sound what skill she hath." (*Retires.*

Re-enter the Bastard of Orleans. leading the steed on which JOAN *is mounted, (a flourish of trumpets,)* JOAN *springs from her saddle.*

Reignier. "Fair maid, is't thou wilt do these wondrous feats?"

Joan. " Reignier, is t thou that thinkest to beguile me ? Where is the Dauphin ?—Come, come from behind : I know thee well, though never seen before. Be not amazed, there's nothing hid from me. In private will I talk to thee apart :—Stand back, you lords, and gives us leave awhile."

Reignier. "She takes upon her bravely at first dash."

Joan. " Dauphin, I am by birth a shepherd's daughter ; my wit untrained in any kind of art. Heaven and my gracious ' mother ' hath it pleased to shine on my contemptible estate. Lo, as I ' slept beneath an oak,' and ' from ' sun's parching heat my cheeks withdrew my ' mother' deigned to appear to me, and in a vision full of majesty willed me to leave my base vocation and free my country from calamity. In complete glory she revealed herself ; and whereas, I was black and swart before, with those clear rays which she infused on me, that beauty am I blessed with which you see. Ask me what question thou can'st possible, and I will answer unpremeditated. My courage try in combat, if thou dar'st, and thou shalt find that I exceed my sex. Resolve on this, thou shalt be fortunate if thou receive me for thy warlike mate."

King Charles. " Thou hast astonished me with thy high terms. Only this proof I'll of thy valour make. In single combat thou shalt buckle with me, and if thou vanquishest, thy words are true ; otherwise I renounce all confidence."

Joan. " I am prepared ; here is my keen-edged sword, decked with five *flower-de-luces* on each side ; the which at Tourraine in Saint Katherine's churchyard, out of a great deal of old iron I chose forth."

King Charles. " Then come ; ' come on ;' I fear no woman."

Joan. " And while I live I'll n'er fly from a man." (*They fight, and* JOAN *overcomes.*)

King Charles. " Stay, stay thy hands, thou art an Amazon, and fightest with the sword of Deborah."

Joan. " My ' mother ' helps me, else I were too weak."

King Charles. "Who'er helps thee 'tis thou that must help me. Impatiently I burn with thy desire. My heart and hands thou hast

at once subdued. Excellent Joan, if thy name be so, let me thy
servant not thy sovereign be. 'Tis the French Dauphin sueth to thee
thus."

Joan. " I must not yield to any rites of love, for my profession's
sacred from above, when I have chased all thy foes from hence,
then will I think upon a recompense."

King Charles. " Meantime look gracious on my prostrate thrall."

Reignier. " My lord, methinks is very long in talk."

Alencon. " Doubtless, he shrives this woman to her smock, else
n'er could he so long protract his speech."

Reignier. " Shall we disturb him, since he keeps no mean ?"

Alencon. " He may mean more than we poor men do know :
these women are shrewd tempters with their tongues."

Reignier. " My lord, where are you ? What devise you on ?
Shall we give Orleans, or no ?"

Joan. " Why, no ! distrustful recreants ! Fight till the last gasp.
I will be your guard."

King Charles. " What she says I will confirm ; we'll fight it out."

Joan. "Assigned am I to be the English scourge. This night the
siege assuredly I'll raise : Expect Saint Martin's summer halcyon
days, since I have entered in these wars. Glory is like a circle in the
water which never ceaseth to enlarge itself, till by broad spreading it
expand to naught. With Henry's death, the English circle ends ;
dispersed are the glories it included. Now am I like that proud, in-
sulting ship which Cæsar and his fortune bare at once."

King Charles. " Was Mahomet inspired with a dove ? Thou
with an eagle art inspired then. Helen, the mother of great Con-
stantine, nor yet Saint Philip's daughters, were like thee. Bright star
of Venus, fall'n down on the earth. How may I reverently worship
thee enough ?"

Alencon. " Leave off delays, and let us raise the siege."

Reignier. " Woman do what thou can'st to save our honours ;
drive them from Orleans, and be immortalized."

King Charles. " Presently we'll try.—Come let's away about it :
No prophet will I trust if she prove false." (*Exeunt.*) (JOAN *bows*

*to the King and some of his men as they pass out; then makes a signal
to the Bastard of Orleans to help her mount her steed.*)

Joan. Arise! away! to kill the vultures floating 'neath thefr own
of Heaven. Ay, vultures who'ed clutch the hearts of mothers, make
their children carrion, soil the flags of honor, capture our maids to
serve as sensual feasts, swallow our gold, then dance to hear it ring.
Sack all the wealth of France, then rest on bloody seas from toils of
war. Awake, arise, arise, ye gallant sons of France, and angels pros-
per Joan till she win the day. Away! Away! (JOAN *rides off, the
soldiers follow her.*)

SCENE III.—*Rouen. Enter* JOAN, *disguised, and soldiers, dressed like
peasants, with sacks on their backs.*

Joan. "These are the city gates, the gates of Rouen, through
which our policy must make a breach. Take heed, be wary, how
you place your words; talk like the vulgar sort of market-men that
come to gather money for their corn. If we have entrance (as I hope
we shall.) and that we find the slothful watch but weak, I'll by a sign
give notice to our friends, that Charles the Dauphin may encounter
them."

A Soldier. "Our sacks shall be a means to sack this city, and we
be lords and rulers over Rouen. Therefore we will knock."

(*Knocks.*)

Guard. (*within*) "Qui est la?"
Joan. "Paisans pauvres, gens de France. Poor market-folks,
that come to sell their corn."
Guard. "Enter, go in, the market bell is rung." (*Opens the gate.*)
Joan. "Now, Rouen, I'll shake thy bulwarks to the ground."
![(Joan and soldiers enter the city.*)

42

Enter CHARLES, *King of France*; *the* BASTARD OF ORLEANS; *the* DUKE OF ALENCON: REIGNIER; DUKE OF ANJOU; *and Forces.*

King Charles. "Saint Denis bless this happy stratagem! and once again we'll sleep secure in Rouen."

Bastard. "Here entered Joan and her partisans. Now she is there, how will she specify where is the best and safest passage in?"

Reignier. "By thrusting out a torch from yonder tower, which, once discerned, shows that her meaning is: no way to that for weakness which she entered."

Enter JOAN, *on a battlement, holding out a torch burning.*

Joan. "Behold, this is the happy wedding torch that joineth Rouen unto her countrymen, but burning fatal to the Talbotites."

Bastard. "See, noble Charles! the beacon of our friend, the burning torch in yonder turret stands."

King Charles. "Now shines it like a comet of revenge, a prophet to the fall of all our foes!"

Reignier. "Defer no time; delays have dangerous ends. Enter, and cry, THE DAUPHIN,! presently and then do execution on the watch." (*They enter the town.*)

SCENE IV.—*Enter from the town, the* DUKE OF BEDFORD, *brought in sick on a chair, with* EARL TALBOT, *the* DUKE OF BURGUNDY, *and the English Forces. Then enter on the walls,* JOAN, KING CHARLES, THE BASTARD, *the* DUKE OF ALENCON, REIGNIER, *and others.*

Joan. "Good morrow, gallants! want ye corn for bread? I think the Duke of Burgundy will fast before he'll buy again at such a rate, 'Twas full of darnel, do you like the taste?"

Bur. "Scoff on, vile fiend, and shameless courtezan. I trust ere long to choke thee with thine own, and make thee curse the haruest of that corn."

King Charles. " Your grace may perhaps starve before that time."

Bed. " O let not words, but deeds, revenge this treason! "

Joan. What will you do, good gray-beard? break a lance, and run a tilt at death within a chair? "

Talbot. " Foul fiend of France, and hag of all, despite encompassed with thy lustful paramours, becomes it thee to taunt his valiant age, and twit with cowardice a man half dead? Damsel, I'll have a bout with you again, or else let Talbot perish with his shame."

Joan. " Are you so hot, sir? Yet, Joan, hold thy peace; if Talbot do but thunder, rain will follow." (*Talbot and the rest consult together.*)

Talbot. " Dare ye come forth, and meet us in the field? "

Joan. " Belike your lordship takes us then for fools to try if that our own be ours or no."

Talbot. " I speak not to that railing Hecaté, but unto thee, Alencon, and the rest. Will ye, like soldiers, come and fight it out? "

Alencon. " Signior, no."

Talbot. " Signior, hang! base muleteers of France! like peasant footboys, do they keep the walls, and dare not take up arms, like gentlemen."

Joan. " Away, captains; let's get us from the walls, for Talbot means no goodness by his looks." Good luck to you, my lord! " We came but to tell you that we are here." (*Exeunt* JOAN *and the soldiers from the walls.*)

Talbot. " And there we will be, too, ere it be long, or else reproach be Talbot's greatest fame. Vow, Burgundy, by honour of thy house, pricked on by public wrongs sustained in France, either to get the town again or die. And I, as sure as English Henry lives, and as his father here was conqueror,—as sure as in this late betrayed town, great COEUR DE LION's heart was buried,—so sure I swear to get the town or die." (*Exeunt.*

Scene V.—*The last battle between the French and English. The French defeated. Scene, the town of Angiers.*

Enter JOAN.

Joan. "The Regent conquers, and the Frenchmen fly. Now, help, ye charming spells, and periapts; and ye choice spirits that admonish me, and give me signs of future accidents! (*Thunder.*) You speedy helpers, that are substitutes under the lordly monarch of the North, appear and aid me in my enterprise!

Enter FIENDS.

Joan. "This speedy, quick appearance argues proof of your accustomed diligence to me. Now, ye familiar spirits, that are called out of the powerful regions under earth, help me this once that France may get the field." (*They walk about and speak not.*) "O hold me not with silence over long! Where I was wont to feed you with my blood, I'll lop a member off, and give it you in earnest of a further benefit; so you do condescend to help me now." (*They hang their heads.*) "No hope to have redress? My body shall pay recompense if you will grant my suit." (*They shake their heads.*) "Cannot my body, nor blood-sacrifice, entreat you to your wonted furtherance? Then take my soul, my body, soul and all, before that England give the French the foil." (*They depart.*) "See! now the time is come that France must vail her lofty-plumèd crest, and let her head fall into England's lap. My ancient incantations are too weak, and hell too strong for me to buckle with: now, France, thy glory droopeth to the dust." (*Exit.*

Alarums. Enter French and English fighting, JOAN *and* YORK *fighting hand to hand.* JOAN *is taken. The French fly.*

York. " Damsel of France, I think I have you fast; unchain your spirits now with spelling charms and try if they can gain your liberty. A goodly prize, fit for the devil's grace ! See how the ugly witch doth bend her brows, as if with Circe she would change my shape."

Joan. "Changed to a worser shape thou canst not be."

York. " O, Charles, the Dauphin, is the proper man : No shape but his can please your dainty eye."

Joan. " A plaguing mischief light on Charles and thee ! and may ye both be suddenly surprised by bloody hands in sleeping on your beds!"

York. " Fell, banning hag ! Enchantress, hold thy tongue."

Joan. " I pr'ythee give me leave to curse awhile."

York. " Curse, miscreant, when thou comest to the stake."

(*Exeunt.*

SCENE VI.—*A market place in the town of Rouen.* JOAN *tied to a stake. Flames burning around her, her arms charred, and streaked with blood and gore. At intervals she shrieks with pain, or groans in agony. A mob and soldiers of the British forces stand looking at her. She pronounces a curse upon England and dies.*

Joan. The curse that creeps from out the jaws of Death, all heavy curses I now pluck from out my grave. Down, down, from that drear cold abyss I fetch those venomed stings for England's head. May all the other countries that round England lie, rise in one mighty army under some pretense, and war disable her; turn her a hunch-back with four dangling limbs, and leave her seated thus to mourn her foulsome state. Thus seated, to think and weep o'er endless woes; pine o'er her dull captivity; like some huge monster wasting all its days in gnawing for its flight ; gnawing back on self, same spots to gnaw again; and with that gnawing but to gnaw in vain; thus with all curses more that any can invent, my soul breaks from its seat. Away! Away! Shake off this dusty mould, France, France,—I'm free,—I'm free. (*Dies. The soldiers, when they see* JOAN *is dead, propose a "Wake." The mob drink wine, and break bottles, a general confusion takes place. The soldiers join hands and dance round the body of* JOAN *singing a song.*)

Leader of the soldiers. Come, lets join hands and have a song, and all who're in the limits of a mile hie to the "Wake." (*The soldiers dance and sing.*)

Hi, ho, the witch is dead, the witch is dead ;
The witch is dead, hi, ho,
The witch is dead, hi, ho, hi, ho, hi, ho.

CURTAIN FALLS.

END.

www.ingramcontent.com/pod-product-compliance
Lightning Source LLC
Chambersburg PA
CBHW030909260626
47169CB00008B/2769